TIPS TO SUPPORT LITERACY AT HOME

WHY READING AND SINGING WITH YOUR CHILD IS SO IMPORTANT

Daily reading with your child leads to increased academic achievement. Music and songs, specifically rhyming songs, are a fun and easy way to build early literacy and language development. Music skills correlate significantly with both phonological awareness and reading development. Singing helps build vocabulary and speech development. And reading and appreciating music together is a wonderful way to strengthen your relationship.

READ AND SING EVERY DAY!

TIPS FOR USING CANTATA LEARNING BOOKS AND SONGS DURING YOUR DAILY STORY TIME

1. As you sing and read, point out the different words on the page that rhyme. Suggest other words that rhyme.
2. Memorize simple rhymes such as Itsy Bitsy Spider and sing them together. This encourages comprehension skills and early literacy skills.
3. Use the questions in the back of each book to guide your singing and storytelling.
4. Read the included sheet music with your child while you listen to the song. How do the music notes correlate to the words of the song?
5. Sing along on the go and at home. Access music by scanning the QR code on each Cantata book. You can also stream or download the music for free to your computer, smartphone, or mobile device.

Devoting time to daily reading shows that you are available for your child. Together, you are building language, literacy, and listening skills.

Have fun reading and singing!

Halloween is October 31. It is also the night before All Saints Day, or All Hallows Day. Long ago, children would go guising on Halloween. They dressed up in costumes and went door to door. People gave them gifts of food and money. Today, this tradition is known as trick-or-treating.

To learn what makes Halloween the scariest holiday of the year, turn the page and sing along!

HALLOWEEN

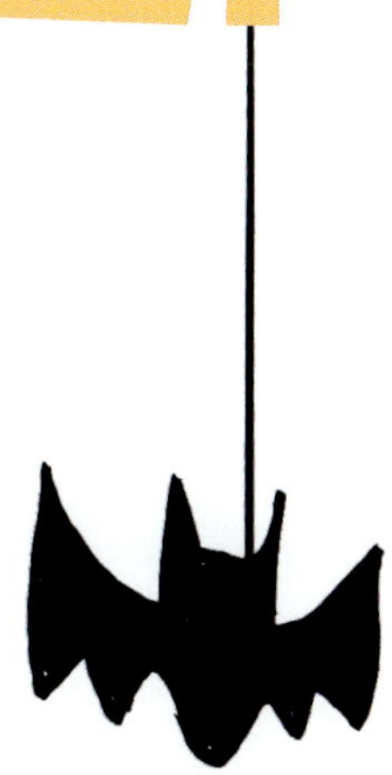

By ALLAN MOREY

Illustrations by DOREEN MULRYAN

Music by MARK OBLINGER

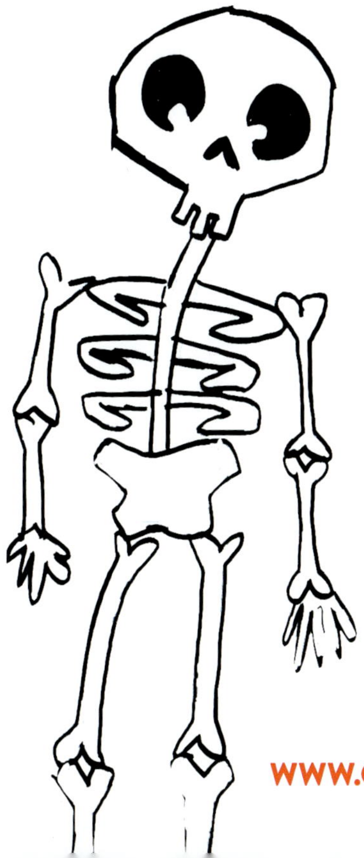

CANTATA LEARNING

WWW.CANTATALEARNING.COM

CANTATA
LEARNING

Published by Cantata Learning
1710 Roe Crest Drive
North Mankato, MN 56003
www.cantatalearning.com

Library of Congress Cataloging-in-Publication Data
Names: Morey, Allan, author. | Mulryan, Doreen, illustrator. | Oblinger, Mark (Composer)
Title: Halloween / by Allan Morey ; illustrations by Doreen Mulryan ; music by Mark Oblinger.
Description: North Mankato, Minnesota : Cantata Learning, [2018] | Series: Holidays in Rhythm and Rhyme | "Music direction: Elizabeth Draper, Music written and produced by Mark Oblinger"--T.p. verso. | This is a sing along book in rhyme. | Audience: Ages: 5-8. | Audience: Grades: K to Grade 3. |
Identifiers: LCCN 2017007518 (print) | LCCN 2017016344 (ebook) | ISBN 9781684100323 | ISBN 9781684100316 (hardcover : alk. paper)
Subjects: LCSH: Halloween--Juvenile literature. | Halloween--Songs and music.
Classification: LCC GT4965 (ebook) | LCC GT4965 .M664 2018 (print) | DDC 394.2646--dc23
LC record available at https://lccn.loc.gov/2017007518

978-1-68410-280-8 (paperback)

Book design, Tim Palin Creative
Editorial direction, Flat Sole Studio
Executive musical production and direction, Elizabeth Draper
Music arranged and produced by Mark Oblinger

Printed in the United States of America.
0401

ACCESS THE MUSIC!
SCAN CODE WITH MOBILE APP
CANTATALEARNING.COM

Come celebrate Halloween,
the holiday that makes us scream.

Tonight, scary monsters walk the streets.
They are looking for tasty treats.

Pirates dance and witches laugh,

"It's time to trick-or-treat!"

Vampires prowl and **werewolves** howl,

"Tonight is Halloween!"

SCHOOL
HAUNTED HOUSE
RIP
HERE LIES

Come creep quietly as a mouse
through a spooky haunted house.

See the bats flapping their wings
and bowls of gross, icky things.

Pirates dance and witches laugh,
"It's time to trick-or-treat!"

Vampires prowl and werewolves howl,
"Tonight is Halloween!"

Come and see, glowing in the night,
jack-o'-lanterns causing a fright.

HALLOWEEN

By ALLAN MOREY
Illustrations by DOREEN MULRYAN
Music by MARK OBLINGER

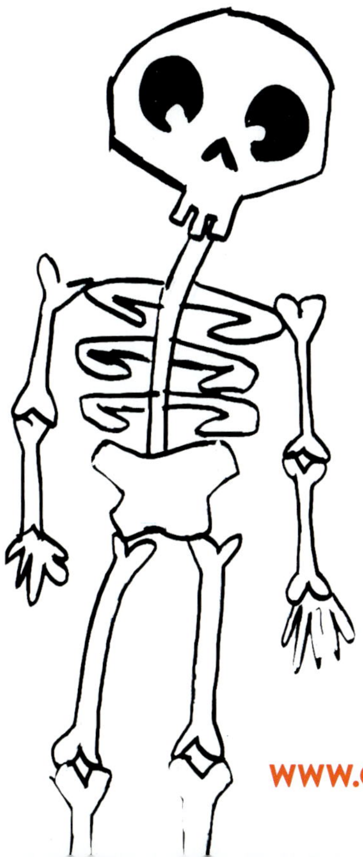

CANTATA LEARNING

WWW.CANTATALEARNING.COM

Published by Cantata Learning
1710 Roe Crest Drive
North Mankato, MN 56003
www.cantatalearning.com

Library of Congress Cataloging-in-Publication Data
Names: Morey, Allan, author. | Mulryan, Doreen, illustrator. | Oblinger, Mark (Composer)
Title: Halloween / by Allan Morey ; illustrations by Doreen Mulryan ; music by Mark Oblinger.
Description: North Mankato, Minnesota : Cantata Learning, [2018] | Series: Holidays in Rhythm and Rhyme | "Music direction: Elizabeth Draper, Music written and produced by Mark Oblinger"--T.p. verso. | This is a sing along book in rhyme. | Audience: Ages: 5-8. | Audience: Grades: K to Grade 3. |
Identifiers: LCCN 2017007518 (print) | LCCN 2017016344 (ebook) | ISBN 9781684100323 | ISBN 9781684100316 (hardcover : alk. paper)
Subjects: LCSH: Halloween--Juvenile literature. | Halloween--Songs and music.
Classification: LCC GT4965 (ebook) | LCC GT4965 .M664 2018 (print) | DDC 394.2646--dc23
LC record available at https://lccn.loc.gov/2017007518

978-1-68410-280-8 (paperback)

Book design, Tim Palin Creative
Editorial direction, Flat Sole Studio
Executive musical production and direction, Elizabeth Draper
Music arranged and produced by Mark Oblinger

Printed in the United States of America.
0401

ACCESS THE MUSIC!
SCAN CODE WITH MOBILE APP
CANTATALEARNING.COM

Spiderwebs hang all around,
and skeleton bones
lie on the ground.

Pirates dance and witches laugh,
"It's time to trick-or-treat!"

Vampires prowl and werewolves howl,
"Tonight is Halloween!"

Come trick-or-treat with scary **ghouls**,
princesses, and cowboys, oh so cool!

There are many costumes to see,
like superheroes and **zombies**.

Pirates dance and witches laugh,
"It's time to trick-or-treat!"

Vampires prowl and werewolves howl,
"Tonight is Halloween!"

(Boo) It's time to trick-or-treat!
Tonight is Halloween!

(Boo) It's time to trick-or-treat!
Tonight is Halloween!

SONG LYRICS
Halloween

Come celebrate Halloween,
the holiday that makes us scream.
Tonight, scary monsters walk the streets.
They are looking for tasty treats.

Pirates dance and witches laugh,
"It's time to trick-or-treat!"
Vampires prowl and werewolves howl,
"Tonight is Halloween!"

Come creep quietly as a mouse
through a spooky haunted house.
See the bats flapping their wings
and bowls of gross, icky things.

Pirates dance and witches laugh,
"It's time to trick-or-treat!"
Vampires prowl and werewolves howl,
"Tonight is Halloween!"

Come and see, glowing in the night,
jack-o'-lanterns causing a fright.
Spiderwebs hang all around,
and skeleton bones lie on the ground.

Pirates dance and witches laugh,
"It's time to trick-or-treat!"
Vampires prowl and werewolves howl,
"Tonight is Halloween!"

Come trick-or-treat with scary ghouls,
princesses, and cowboys, oh, so cool!
There are many costumes to see,
like superheroes and zombies.

Pirates dance and witches laugh,
"It's time to trick-or-treat!"
Vampires prowl and werewolves howl,
"Tonight is Halloween!"

(Boo) It's time to trick-or-treat!
Tonight is Halloween!

(Boo) It's time to trick-or-treat!
Tonight is Halloween!

Halloween

Rock and Roll
Mark Oblinger

Verse

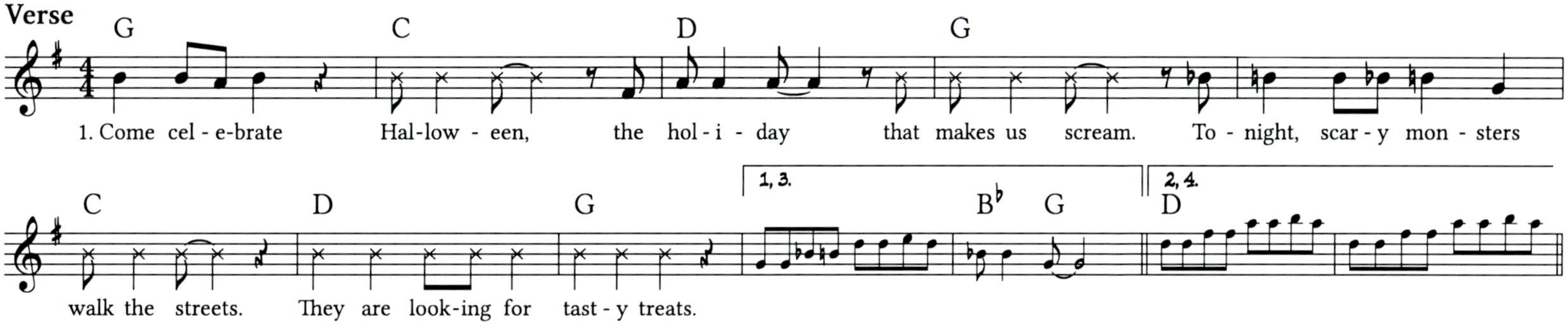

Chorus

Verse 2
Come creep quietly as a mouse
through a spooky haunted house.
See the bats flapping their wings
and bowls of gross, icky things.

Chorus

Verse 3
Come and see, glowing in the night,
jack-o'-lanterns causing a fright.
Spiderwebs hang all around,
and skeleton bones lie on the ground.

Chorus

Verse 4
Come trick-or-treat with scary ghouls,
princesses, and cowboys, oh, so cool!
There are many costumes to see,
like superheroes and zombies.

Chorus

Outro

ACCESS THE MUSIC!
SCAN CODE WITH MOBILE APP
CANTATALEARNING.COM

GLOSSARY

ghouls—undead creatures who rob graves and eat the dead

vampires—undead creatures who drink the blood of people

werewolves—people who can turn into wolves

zombies—people who are dead but can still walk around

GUIDED READING ACTIVITIES

1. This book showed you a lot of kids in costumes. Can you remember some of them? Which costume did you like the best? Draw a picture of it.

2. Have you ever been trick-or-treating? What kinds of candy did you get? What was your favorite? Do you get candy on any other holidays?

3. It's never too early to start planning for Halloween. What would you like to dress up as next Halloween? What kind of clothes would you need to make your costume? What other things would you need?

TO LEARN MORE

Appleby, Alex. *Happy Halloween!* New York: Gareth Stevens, 2014.

Felix, Rebecca. *We Celebrate Halloween in Fall.* Ann Arbor, MI: Cherry Lake, 2013.

Griswold, Cliff. *Dressing Up for Halloween.* New York: Gareth Stevens, 2015.

Marsh, Laura F. *Halloween.* Washington, DC: National Geographic Society, 2012.